Fuzzy Rabbit

A Random House PICTUREBACK®

FOR BETTY

Fuzzy Rabbit

by Rosemary Billam

Pictures by Vanessa Julian-Ottie

RANDOM HOUSE 🏠 NEW YORK

First American Edition, 1984.
Text copyright © 1982 by Rosemary Billam. Illustrations copyright © 1982 by Vanessa Julian-Ottie. All rights reserved under International and Pan-American Copyright Conventions. Published in the United States by Random House, Inc., New York. Originally published in Great Britain as ALPACA by William Collins Sons & Co. Ltd., Glasgow, in 1982.
Library of Congress Cataloging in Publication Data: Billam, Rosemary. Fuzzy Rabbit. (A Random House pictureback) SUMMARY: As Fuzzy Rabbit's mistress gets other newer toys, he begins to feel neglected and unloved. [1. Toys—Fiction. 2. Rabbits—Fiction] I. Julian-Ottie, Vanessa, ill. II. Title. PZ7.B494Fu 1984 [E] 83-17637 ISBN: 0-394-86346-1 (trade); 0-394-96346-6 (lib. bdg.)
Manufactured in the United States of America

19 20

Fuzzy Rabbit had been with the family for as long as he could remember. His dungarees were faded. He had a hole in the elbow of his sweater, and his buttons were all odd ones of different sizes. One of the stitches of his mouth had come undone, and he couldn't even smile.

His little girl, Ellen, kept telling him to cheer up. He tried, but he felt lonely and down in the dumps.

He remembered the old days when Ellen used
to take him to school in her knapsack. That was
interesting. He liked learning things. He liked
the other children.

He used to sit next to Ellen
and help her with her math,

and watch her paint.

But recently Ellen had started leaving
him at home with the other toys.

On her birthday, for the first time, Ellen forgot to take Fuzzy downstairs for her birthday party. He could hear the children in the front room, dancing to music and playing games. He sighed. He felt a bit left out. He decided to go and have a little peek, so he climbed off the bed and tiptoed out to the landing.

He lowered himself down the stairs and
pushed his head between the banister rails.

He could see Ellen opening her presents.
There were pieces of wrapping paper and bits
of ribbon and cards and envelopes all over
the floor. Fuzzy had never seen so many
presents.

There were cries of delight as Ellen opened a
box and took out a pink doll with curly hair
and shiny black shoes.

Fuzzy thought that she looked like a
perfectly ordinary sort of doll.

Ellen was excitedly opening her next present.
Inside was a feathery owl wearing a pair of
spectacles. Ellen showed him off to her friends.
Fuzzy couldn't see what all the fuss was
about.

Ellen's mother started to light the candles on
the cake.

"I'll just shut the door so that the draft
won't blow them out," she said.

It was dark and cold on the landing and
Fuzzy couldn't watch the party anymore, so
he went back to Ellen's room and climbed up
on the bed. He kept thinking what a lot of fun
the children were having.

That night Ellen was allowed to stay up late.
When it was time for bed, she had to get out
of her party dress and into her nightgown very
quickly. She put the pink doll and the owl
onto her bed next to Fuzzy.

"Move over, Fuzzy," she said.

Fuzzy wished the new toys didn't take up so much room. He nudged the owl to make him move over a bit. The owl pecked him. Fuzzy didn't think that was very polite.

Fuzzy hoped Ellen would see that he was being squashed, but after saying good night, she went straight to sleep because she was so tired.

"Excuse me," he whispered to the pink doll, "but I need a bit more space." She pretended not to hear him. Fuzzy gave her a push, but she pushed him back and Fuzzy fell over the side and rolled underneath the bed.

It was very cold on the floor all night but, what was worse, nobody noticed that he was missing in the morning. He lay there sadly all day, sneezing in the dust. Nobody heard him. Fuzzy wondered if Ellen would remember him when she came home from school. Would she think of looking under the bed?

At four o'clock Ellen's friend Mary came
over to play.

"What shall we do this afternoon?" asked
Mary.

"Let's play nurses," said Ellen.

They got out Ellen's nursing kit and uniform
from the dresser.

The girls put all the toys into the hospital,
but Ellen wasn't happy. Something wasn't right.
Something was missing.

"Where's Fuzzy?" she said.

The girls searched in the closet, behind
the curtains, and under the bedcovers.

"He's lost," said Mary.

"He must be hiding," said Ellen. She looked under the bed.

"Fuzzy! What are you doing down there? You're all dusty."

Ellen picked Fuzzy up and gave him a hug.

Ellen was surprised at how thin he'd become.

"I remember when Mommy first made you. You were so cuddly and cheerful and bright," she said. She looked at Fuzzy and noticed that the fuzzy wool on his face had worn away and that he was losing some of his stuffing. "Look," she whispered to Mary.

"I could take him home with me and make him better," said Mary. "I'd swap my kaleidoscope for him," she added.

Fuzzy was suddenly very frightened. Mary was quite a nice little girl but he didn't want to go and live at her house. What would Ellen say?

Ellen didn't need time to think.
She answered right away.

"I wouldn't swap Fuzzy for anything. He's always been my best friend. I can make him better."

Fuzzy felt happy through and through.

Mary took his temperature and made charts for all the other patients while Ellen threaded a needle for the operation. She got the syringe out of her nursing kit and gave Fuzzy an injection. "It won't hurt now," she told him.

Ellen pushed all his stuffing back in and sewed him up. "All over now!" she said.

She also put another stitch in his lips so that he could smile again. Ellen and Fuzzy smiled at each other.

Ellen fussed over Fuzzy while Mary gave the owl some medicine and tied a bandage around the pink doll's arm.

"What are their names?" asked Mary.

"They haven't got names yet," said Ellen.

Fuzzy looked across at the new toys, sitting in the old cradle. He thought how horrible it must be not to have a name.

"What are you going to call them?" asked Mary.

"I'll call the owl Wisey because he's wise and I'll call the doll Jane because . . . she looks like a Jane," said Ellen.

Ellen's mother called, "Tea's ready," so the girls ran downstairs. Fuzzy went over to Jane and Wisey.

"Hello," he said. "My name's Fuzzy."

Just then the door opened, and Ellen and
Mary came back. They sat all the toys down
in a circle and set out the dolls' tea service.
Mary poured the orange juice and Ellen
sliced the birthday cake. She gave Fuzzy
the biggest piece because he'd been so brave.

"It's nice to have friends," thought Fuzzy,
smiling.